9705

J

Cole, William, 1919-
   Aunt Bella's umbrella. Illus. by Jacqueline
Chwast. ⸢1st ed.⸣ Garden City, N.Y.,
Doubleday, ⸢c1970⸣
   45p. col.illus. 20cm.

I.Title.

RBP

AUNT BELLA'S UMBRELLA

Aunt Bella's Umbrella

By William Cole
Illustrated
by Jacqueline
Chwast

9705

I remember Aunt Bella's umbrella.

Some people have tiny umbrellas,
and they can't share them.

Others have regular umbrellas,
but they're too selfish to share them.

And still others will *some*times share,
but they'll let the other person get half wet.

Aunt Bella didn't want *any*body *ever* to get wet,
and whenever it started to rain she'd say,
"Timmie! It's umbrella time!"
And we'd put on our yellow slickers
and our black galoshes
and out we'd go!

Whenever Aunt Bella saw anybody ducking from the rain
and hiding in doorways, she'd cry,
"There's one! Come on in under here and get dry!"

"Ah, there's another poor wet soul," she'd say to me. Then she'd shout, "Come on in under! Come on in under!"

And I'd yell, "Oh, there's another! Yoo-hoo, you over there—
come on in under Aunt Bella's umbrella!"

And we'd gather quite a crowd.
The rain would be pelting down,
the drops bouncing
from the road,
and the wind would
be whipping around,
and we'd all huddle
close to one another,
with that wonderful
feeling

. . . like being in a cottage at the beach and
hearing the rain on the roof

. . . like being in a warm,
snug boat, rolling with
the storm

. . . like riding in an automobile
through the rain,
under a rug,
with the windshield wipers
click-clacking.

There'd be five people and six and ten
and eleven. "Always room for one more poor
wet soul," Aunt Bella would shout

and the umbrella seemed to grow bigger and
bigger. There was always room for everybody,
and we'd all chant my umbrella song,

"We don't care if you're a girl or a fella,
If you're Stella, Louella, or Della,
If you're brown or you're white or you're yella,
Come in under Aunt Bella's umbrella!"

We'd march around
town, singing and laughing
and feeling
close to one another,

and new people would join us, and others would drop off

and leave when they came to their homes,
or to the stores where they wanted to shop.

They'd wave good-by.

"*Thank* you, Aunt Bella!"
"*Bless* you, Aunt Bella!"

until there was only us again
and it was like any other umbrella.

We'd come back home,
tired and happy, and take off our
yellow slickers
and our black galoshes,

and have cocoa and cookies.

Aunt Bella would stretch and yawn and say
"Those poor wet souls . . ."
And bit by bit she'd fall off to sleep in her chair, and I
could hear her mutter softly, ". . . Those poor wet souls . . .
those poor wet souls . . ."

WILLIAM COLE spent 20 years as a publisher before deciding to devote his full time to writing and editing. Since then he has been far from idle, having produced more than thirty anthologies and any number of children's stories.

He lives in New York City and has three children.

JACQUELINE CHWAST is a graduate of the Art High School of Newark, New Jersey and of the Newark School of Fine and Industrial Arts.

Mrs. Chwast divides her time between her illustration work and running a household which includes her husband (also an illustrator) and their two daughters.

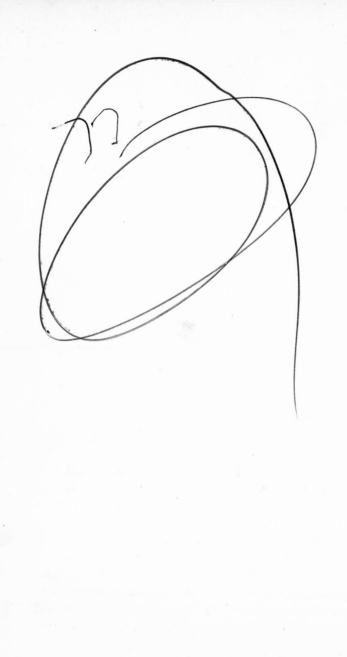